For Janet Lily Sislowitz
—J. Y.

For my friend, Abby
—D. A.

ISBN 978-0-545-64303-0

Text copyright © 2012 by Jane Yolen. Illustrations copyright © 2012 by Derek Anderson. All rights reserved. Published by Scholastic Inc., 557 Broadway, New York, NY 10012, by arrangement with Simon & Schuster Books for Young Readers, an imprint of Simon & Schuster Children's Publishing Division. SCHOLASTIC and associated logos are trademarks and/or registered trademarks of Scholastic Inc.

12 11 10 9 8 7 6 5 4 3 2 1   13 14 15 16 17 18/0

Printed in the U.S.A.   40

First Scholastic printing, October 2013

Book design by Chloë Foglia
The text for this book is set in Garamond.
The illustrations for this book are rendered in acrylic paint.

WAKING
DRAGONS

BY JANE YOLEN

PAINTINGS BY DEREK ANDERSON

SCHOLASTIC INC.

Dragons wake up,

dragons rise.

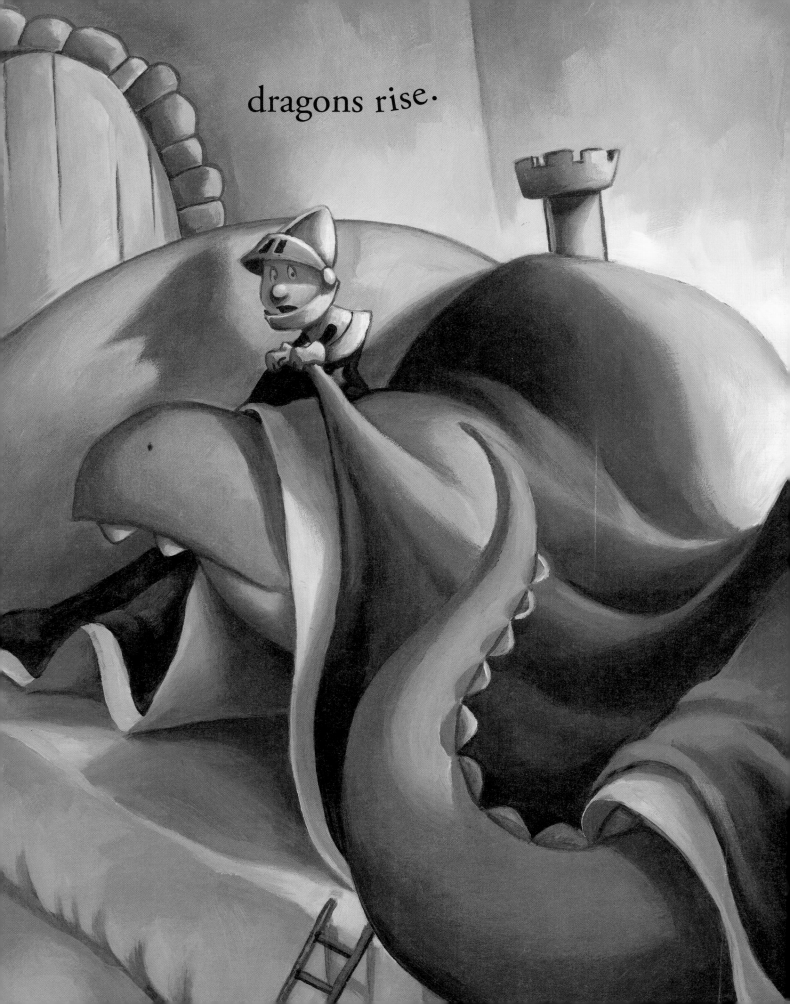

Dragons open
dragon eyes.

Dragons blink,
dragons bumble,

dragons leap,
dragons tumble
out of bed

to brush their teeth,
the fangs above,
the fangs beneath.

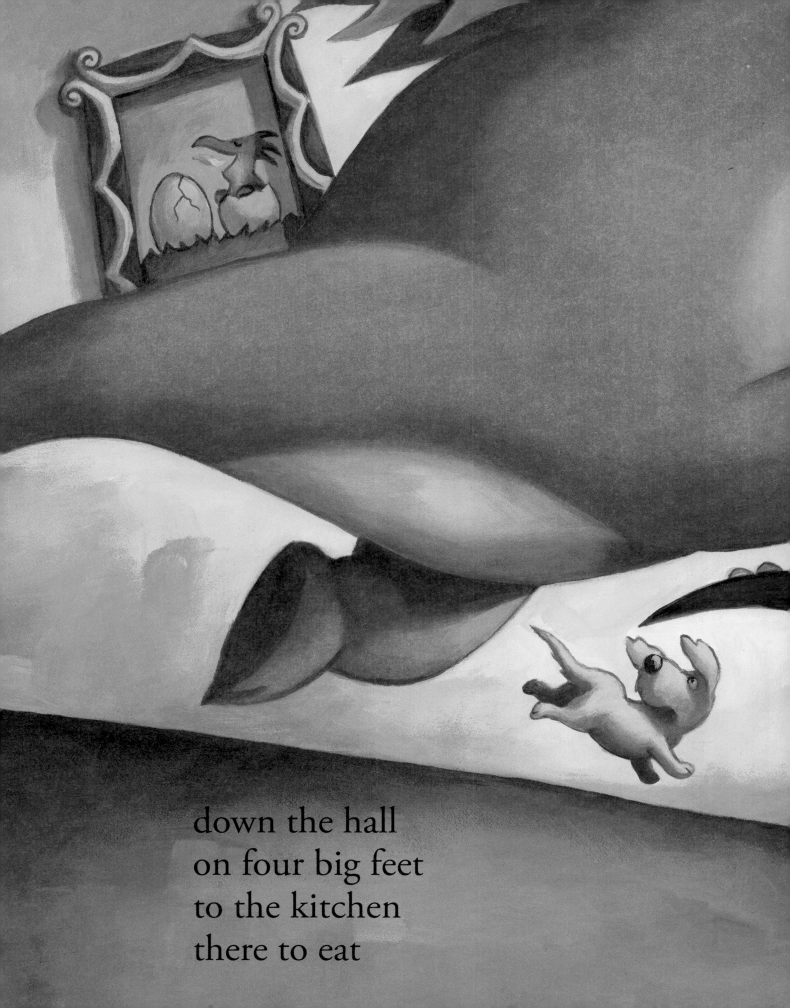

down the hall
on four big feet
to the kitchen
there to eat

breakfast waffles,
topped with syrup,
which makes dragons
really cheer up.

Wipe their faces,
runny noses,

Put their jammies
in the hamper.

Then all dragons
skip and scamper

get into their
outdoor clothes-es.

Kiss their dragon
mom good-bye.
Leap from cave
into the sky,

where dragons
get to fly.

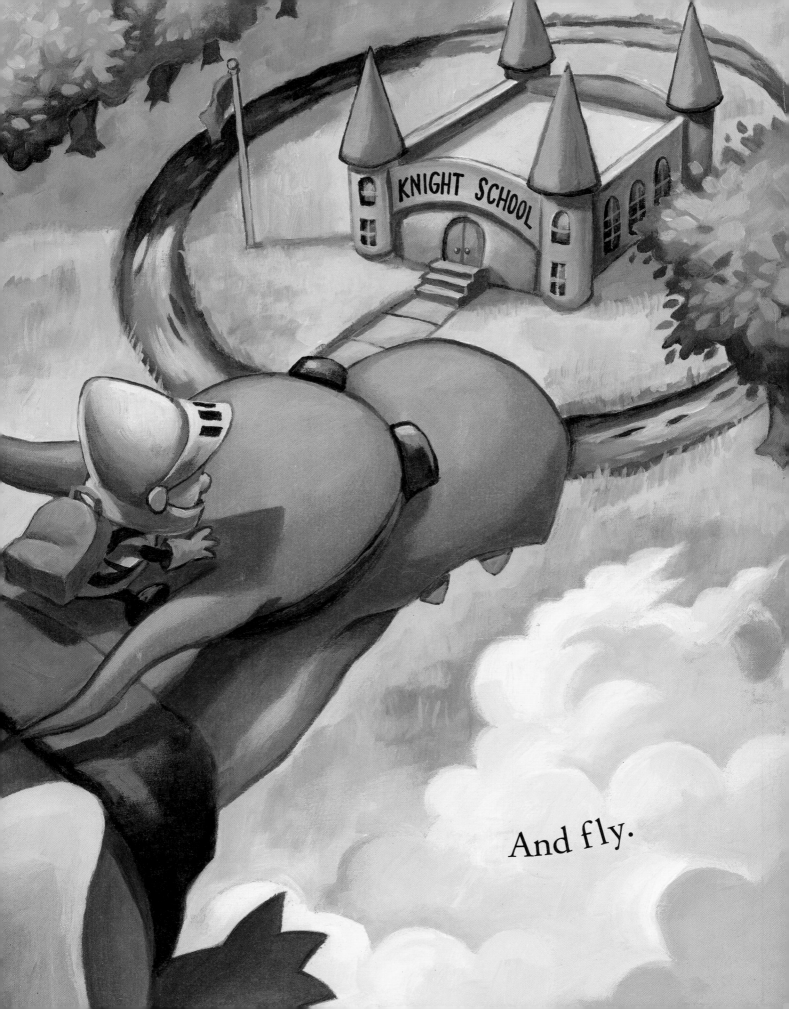

And fly.

And fly.